My Weird School Special

The Leprechaun Is Finally Gone!

Pictures by
Dan Gutman   **Jim Paillot**

HARPER
An Imprint of HarperCollinsPublishers

To Emma

Special thanks to fans who helped teach me about Saint Patrick's Day: Laura Meeker Korch, Kristina Krengel, Daniel Reilly, Rachael Alford, Colleen McAteer Baumgardner, Jessica Beasley, Susie Biondo, Gina D'Angelo Williams, Emily Ebner, Alysa Gayle, Joy Seres-Kilmurray, Erika Maria, Sara Marshall, Kathleen Gilbert Nangle, Aisling O'Donovan, Jenny O'Sullivan, Sinead Queenborg McDonnell Borgersen, Katie Carpenter Smith, Barbara Sorensen Smole, Sara Van Den Bosch, Julie Bastean Yepsen, Allison Kamen, Tracy Hengst, Debi Krueger Hart, Carlie Weaver, Sonya Williams, Sunny Turner, Katie Feighery Hunnes, Stacy Davidson Minicucci, Colleen Neff, Sangita Biniwale Pradhan, Julie Bradford, Allen Thurlow, Diane Donnelly Sperfslage.

Library of Congress Control Number: 2021936554
ISBN 978-0-06-306727-1 (pbk bdg) — ISBN 978-0-06-306728-8 (trade bdg)

Typography by Martha Maynard
21 22 23 24 25   PC/BRR   10 9 8 7 6 5 4 3 2 1
❖
First Edition

Contents

Jake the Snake

My name is A.J. and I know what you're thinking. You're thinking that you're reading this book.

You're thinking that you're reading this sentence.

Now you're thinking that you're reading *this* sentence.

And now you're thinking that you're reading *THIS* sentence.

But what if you're not reading this book at all? What if you're really asleep right now and you're *dreaming* that you're reading this book? Hmmm?

Or what if this book is really reading *you*?

Or what if you're really holding a magic chicken in your hands that can turn itself into the shape of a book, and you're reading a chicken?

Okay, that would be weird.

The point is, it was March. And you know what *that* means—Saint Patrick's Day! It was just one week away.

Our class was sitting in the Book Nook of the library at Ella Mentry School. It was story time with our librarian, Mrs. Roopy. She was finishing a picture book called *The Legend of Saint Patrick*.

". . . and that's the story of how Saint Patrick drove the snakes out of Ireland," read Mrs. Roopy.

She closed the book and we all clapped, because that's what you're supposed to do when anybody finishes anything. Nobody knows why.

"Any questions?" asked Mrs. Roopy.

Andrea Young, this annoying girl with curly brown hair, raised her hand. *Of*

course. Andrea *always* raises her hand. I
bet that the minute she was born, the first
thing Andrea did was raise her hand to
ask the doctor a question.

"Yes, Andrea?" asked Mrs. Roopy.

"Well, I'm half Irish," Andrea said.

"Which half?" I asked. "Top or bottom?"

"Arlo!" shouted Andrea. She calls me by my real name because she knows I don't like it.

"Left or right half?" I asked.

"Please let Andrea speak, A.J.," said Mrs. Roopy.

"My mother told me that the story about Saint Patrick never really happened," said Andrea. "He didn't drive the snakes out of Ireland. My mother said they didn't even *have* snakes in Ireland back in those days."

"Hmmmm," Mrs. Roopy said as she wrinkled up her forehead.

Grown-ups always say "hmmmm" and wrinkle up their foreheads when they don't know what to say. Nobody knows why. But then Mrs. Roopy smiled.

"Wait a minute!" she said excitedly. "This is . . . a teachable moment!"

Oh no. A *boring* moment is more like it.

Grown-ups love teachable moments. That means they get to teach us stuff. And we have to learn stuff. Learning stuff is no fun. That's why I hate teachable moments.

"We can do research!" Mrs. Roopy said as she went over to the computer. "We can find out if Saint Patrick *really* drove the snakes out of Ireland! Let's look it up!"

Oh no! Not research! That's the *worst* kind of teachable moment. Mrs. Roopy loves doing research. She would spend the whole day looking stuff up if she could.

My parents told me that in ancient times

before the internet, primitive humans couldn't just look stuff up on a computer or smartphone. If they wanted to know something, they had to go to the *library*. Ugh! Can you imagine?

So, in the olden days, only smart people knew stuff. These days, *any* dope can look stuff up on a phone and pretend to be smart. It used to be easy to tell who was smart. The smart people knew lots of stuff. Now it's harder to tell who's smart because any dope can look up everything.

Anyway, Mrs. Roopy didn't have the chance to look anything up on the computer because you'll never believe who poked her head into the door at that moment.

Nobody! Why would you poke your head into a door? That would hurt.

But you'll never believe who poked her head into the door*way*.

It was Mrs. Patty, our school secretary! She had a basket in one hand.

"Mrs. Patty!" said Mrs. Roopy. "To what do we owe the pleasure of your company?"

That's grown-up talk for "What are *you* doing here?"

"I heard you talking about Saint Patrick driving the snakes out of Ireland," said Mrs. Patty. "Would you kids like to see something cool?"

"Yes!" we all shouted.

And you'll never believe in a million hundred years what Mrs. Patty was carrying in her basket.

It was a snake!

"Eeeeek!" screamed Michael, who never ties his shoes.

"Help!" shouted Alexia, this girl who rides a skateboard all the time.

"Run for your lives!" shouted Neil, who we call the nude kid even though he wears clothes.

"There's nothing to be afraid of," said Mrs. Patty. "This is my pet snake, Jake. He's my baby."

"HUH?" we all said, which is also "HUH" backward.

Who keeps a snake as a pet? It was ridorkulous.

Mrs. Patty is batty. One Halloween, we

went trick-or-treating at her house. Mrs. Patty had her husband Marvin's head in a bucket down in the basement. But that's a story for another day.

"I *love* Saint Patrick's Day!" said Mrs. Patty. "In fact, my parents were born in Ireland, and they named me Patty after Saint Patrick."

"That snake is scary," whimpered Emily, who's scared of everything.

"Does Jake the Snake bite?" asked Ryan, who will eat anything, even stuff that isn't food.

"Of course not," said Mrs. Patty. "He doesn't have to. He swallows things whole."

WHAT?!

"Just kidding," said Mrs. Patty. "He's an eastern hognose snake. They hardly ever bite. Jake likes people. Who wants to touch him?"

"I do!" said Andrea.

"I do!" I said.

"Oooooh!" said Ryan. "A.J. and Andrea

both said 'I do.' That's what people say when they get married!"

"A.J. and Andrea must be in *love*!" said Michael.

If those guys weren't my best friends, I would hate them.*

---

*Ha-ha! Made you look down!

Top of the Mornin'

Everybody in the class wanted to touch Jake the Snake. Well, almost everybody. There was just one kid who didn't want to touch him. Me! I just *said* I wanted to touch Jake so the guys wouldn't make fun of me.

So I touched Jake. He felt slimy and

creepy and gross. I pretended I liked it.

Mrs. Patty put Jake back in her basket. She was really excited about Saint Patrick's Day coming up.

"You should all wear green, of course," she said, "and we're going to have Irish step dancing, and a four-leaf-clover hunt, and a pickle parade, and . . ."

A pickle parade?

"PicklePalooza," said Mrs. Patty. "I'll tell you all about it next week. For now, I need to go visit the first graders, and Jake needs to eat lunch."

"What does Jake eat for lunch?" asked Alexia.

"First graders!" replied Mrs. Patty.

"Gasp!" we all gasped.

I'm pretty sure Mrs. Patty was kidding about Jake the Snake eating first graders for lunch. After she left, we pringled up and walked a million hundred miles from the library to our classroom.

"I can't wait for Saint Patrick's Day!" Alexia said as we passed by the front office.

"I can," said Andrea. "I don't like Saint Patrick's Day."

What is her problem?

"Maybe we'll see a leprechaun," said Ryan.

"Oooh, I hope so!" said Emily.

"Leprechauns are cool," said Neil.

Huh? A leprechaun?

"What's that?" I asked.

Everybody stopped and looked at me like I farted.

"A.J.," said Michael. "You don't know what a leprechaun is?"

"Uh . . . sure I do," I lied.

Neil whispered in my ear that leprechauns are mischievous little guys who have beards and pull pranks on people. He said that if you catch a leprechaun,

he'll give you a pot of gold he has hidden at the end of a rainbow.

"How do *you* know so much about leprechauns?" I asked Neil.

"I saw one on a box of cereal," he replied.

Everybody was buzzing about leprechauns. But not like bees. That would be weird.*

"There's no such thing as leprechauns," scoffed Andrea. "That's just another Irish stereotype."

"My dad has a type of stereo," I said. Andrea rolled her eyes at me.

We were still talking about leprechauns

*I can't believe you looked down again. The story is up *there*, dumbhead!

17

when we got to the classroom. Our teacher, Mr. Cooper, was waiting for us.

"Okay, everybody," he said as we took our seats. "Let's try to focus this morning."

"Why?" I asked. "We're not cameras."

"Not *that* kind of focus, dumbhead!" Andrea said, rolling her eyes again.

Andrea is always rolling her eyes when I say stuff. I wish her eyes would roll right out of her head.

I wanted to say something mean to Andrea, but I didn't have the chance because Mr. Cooper told us to turn to page twenty-three in our math books. He loves math. I hate it.

I reached into my desk to get out my

math book. But you'll never believe what happened next.

There was a sound in the distance. It was coming from down the hall. It sounded a little bit like geese honking. Or maybe somebody was letting the air out of a giant balloon.

"What's that annoying noise?" asked Alexia.

"It sounds like sheep being tortured," said Ryan, covering his ears.

But it wasn't geese or balloons or sheep being tortured. It was our principal, Mr. Klutz! He was playing the bagpipes, which is a strange musical instrument that's made up of a bunch of pipes sticking out of a bag. So it has the perfect name.

"I know that song!" Andrea said as Mr. Klutz walked into the classroom. "It's 'When Irish Eyes Are Smiling.'"

"Top of the mornin'!" Mr. Klutz said when the song was over. That was weird. Mornings don't have tops or bottoms.

Mr. Klutz took off his green hat and did a little bow. He has no hair at all. I mean *none*. I wonder if hats slip off his head all the time.

"Are you kids excited about Saint Patrick's Day next week?" Mr. Klutz asked.

"Yes!" shouted all the girls.

"No!" shouted all the boys.

I noticed something unusual about Mr. Klutz. He was wearing a skirt!

"Excuse me, Mr. Klutz," I said. "Why are you wearing a skirt today?"

"It's not a skirt, A.J.," he replied. "It's a kilt."

It looked like a skirt to me. Mr. Klutz is nuts.

Andrea looked all mad, as usual.

"They don't wear kilts in Ireland," she said. "They wear kilts in Scotland!"

I didn't even know Ireland and Scotland were different places. I guess Mr. Klutz didn't either.

"I don't feel comfortable with this," Andrea complained. "In Ireland, they don't do any of these silly things on Saint Patrick's Day."

"What *do* they do?" asked Mr. Klutz.

"Saint Patrick's Day is the day Saint Patrick died," Andrea told him. "It's a public holiday. People get the day off. They go to a parade. They go to church. And then they have a big meal. That's it."

"So there are no leprechauns?" asked Emily.

"No," said Andrea.

"No rainbows?" asked Alexia.

"No."

"No pot of gold?" asked Michael.

"No!"

"Saint Patrick's Day in Ireland sounds boring," I said.

Andrea crossed her arms in front of her. That's what people do when they're mad. Nobody knows why.

"Sheesh, lighten up," I told her. Andrea needs to get a sense of humor transplant.

Boycotts and Girlcotts

Finally, it was March 17—Saint Patrick's Day. My mom found a green T-shirt in the back of my closet for me to wear.

When I got to school, it was like the whole world had turned green. Emily was wearing her big sister's green Girl Scout uniform and green ribbons in her hair.

Alexia had painted her toenails and finger-nails green. Neil dyed his hair green. Ryan and his mom walked their dog to school with him, and the *dog* was green!

"What's wrong with your dog?" I asked Ryan.

"We dyed him," he told me.

What? Who dyes a dog?

"Why did you dye your dog?" I asked.

"She's an Irish setter," Ryan explained.

...hat's just weird. Mrs. Patty greeted everybody on the front steps. She was holding Jake the Snake in her basket, and she was dressed head to toe in green, of *course*. She even wore a silly-looking green hat that had a buckle on it.

Why do people have buckles on their hats? I can understand a buckle on your pants. It holds up your pants. I can understand a buckle on your shoes. It holds your shoes together. I guess a buckle on your hat holds your brain together.

Mr. Klutz was wearing a green shirt with the words "Kiss Me, I'm Irish!" on it.*

"I didn't know you were Irish, Mr. Klutz," I said to him.

---

*What's Irish and sits on the porch? Patty O'Furniture!

"*Everybody* is Irish today," he replied. "You can call me Mr. O'Klutz. Or do you think that's going overboard?"

Huh? What do boats have to do with Saint Patrick's Day?

Finally, the bell rang and we went inside. We pringled up and walked a million hundred miles to Mr. Cooper's class. He thinks he's a superhero. He always wears a cape. But on this day, of course, it was a *green* cape. And he told us we should call him Mr. O'Cooper.

"Top of the mornin', everyone," Mr. O'Cooper said cheerfully. "Let's take attendance. Ryan?"

"Here," said Ryan.

"Michael?"

"Here," said Michael.

"A.J.?"

"Not here," I said. "Just kidding. I'm here."

I don't get it. What's the point of taking attendance? If we weren't here, we wouldn't be able to say "here."

"Alexia?"

"Here," said Alexia.

"Neil?"

"Present," said Neil.

Some joker always says "present." What's up with that?

"Andrea?" said Mr. O'Cooper.

Nobody said anything. I turned around. Andrea wasn't in her seat.

"Andrea?" Mr. O'Cooper repeated. "Andrea?"

Andrea was . . . *absent*!

What?! Andrea is *never* absent.

"Hmmm, Andrea must be sick today," said Mr. O'Cooper.

"No, she isn't," said Emily. "Andrea called me this morning. She told me she doesn't approve of the way the school is celebrating Saint Patrick's Day, so she isn't coming in today."

"Wow, Andrea's boycotting school?" Neil said.

"No, she's girlcotting school," I said.

"There's no such thing as girlcotting," said Michael. "Girlcott isn't a word."

"It should be," said Ryan. "How come girls are allowed to boycott, but boys aren't allowed to girlcott? It's not fair!"

"How come boys get a word and girls don't?" said Alexia. "That's not fair either!"

"Yeah!" agreed Emily.

We went on like that for a while, arguing about boycotts and girlcotts.

I was trying to remember the last time Andrea missed school. I think it was on Take Your Daughter to Work Day. That was the greatest day of my life, because Andrea wasn't around to bug me.

"Andrea must be pretty mad about Saint

Patrick's Day," I said.

"Ooooooh!" said Ryan. "You miss Andrea! You must be in *love* with her!"

"When are you and Andrea gonna get married?" asked Michael.

If those guys weren't my best friends, I would hate them.

Good Luck

After we finished arguing, we pledged the allegiance and did Word of the Day. The word of the day was "shamrock." A shamrock is a four-leaf clover that only has three leaves. If you ask me, it should be called a three-leaf clover. Mr. O'Cooper told us the shamrock is the national flower and the emblem of Ireland.

"Should we turn to page twenty-three in our math books?" asked Emily.

"No," said Mr. O'Cooper. "We're not going to do math today."

Yay! I hate math.

"Instead, we're going to learn about Ireland," said Mr. O'Cooper.*

Boo!

Mr. O'Cooper went to the whiteboard and started drawing pictures of shamrocks.

"If four of us each had four shamrocks," he said, "how many shamrocks would we have altogether?"

---

*Do you know why the capital of Ireland is so big? It's been Dublin for years! Get it . . . doublin'?

"Sixteen!" shouted Michael. "Because four times four is sixteen."

"Very good, Michael," said Mr. O'Cooper. "Now try this one. There are about five million Irish people living in Ireland. There are about thirty-two million Irish people living in the United States. How many more Irish people live in the United

States than live in Ireland?"

We all thought that over for a while.

"Twenty-seven million!" shouted Neil.

"Correct!" said Mr. O'Cooper.

"Hey, wait a minute!" I shouted. "You said we weren't going to do math today. This sounds a lot like a math lesson to me."

"No, no. Don't be silly," said Mr. O'Cooper. "We're not learning math. We're learning about Ireland."

Mr. O'Cooper taught us a bunch of other stuff about Ireland, and it all involved addition, subtraction, multiplication, and division. Not fair! When he was done, you'll never believe who came through the door.

Nobody! You can't come through a door. Doors are made of wood. I thought we went over that in Chapter 1. But you'll never believe who came through the door*way.*

It was our music teacher, Mr. Loring! He said we should call him Mr. O'Loring on Saint Patrick's Day, and he started singing a song.

Oh, Danny Boy
The pipes, the pipes are calling . . .

That's a weird song. If your pipes are calling, that means somebody must be stuck in your pipes. You need to call a plumber right away.

"Follow me, everybody," said Mr. O'Loring.

"Where are we going?" Alexia asked.

"You'll find out," Mr. O'Loring replied.

He led us down the hall and out the back door to the playground. Beyond the blacktop is a big grassy area where we play soccer and stuff.

"It's time for our four-leaf-clover hunt!" said Mr. O'Loring.

"Yay!" we all shouted.

Mr. O'Loring told us that each leaf of a four-leaf clover has a meaning—hope, faith, love, and luck. He said four-leaf clovers are really rare. If we found one, he said, it would bring us good luck for the rest of the day.

We got down on our hands and knees and looked for four-leaf clovers. Some of the teachers came out to help—Mr. O'Macky, Miss O'Small, and Mrs. O'Yonkers. Even Mrs. Patty was out there with Jake the Snake in a basket.

"Would you like to touch Jake the Snake?" she asked us.

"We already touched him," I reminded her. "We're looking for four-leaf clovers now."

We searched for a million hundred minutes. There were a lot of clovers with three leaves, but we couldn't find any four-leaf clovers.

That's when I got the greatest idea in the history of the world.

"Hey, Ryan," I whispered. "Why don't we just tear one of the leaves in half so it *looks like* a four-leaf clover?"

"That would be cheating, A.J.," Ryan whispered back. "If you cheat, you'll have *bad* luck for the rest of the day."

What?! No way. What does Ryan know about four-leaf clovers? He's not even Irish. I plucked a three-leaf clover from the grass and carefully tore one of the leaves so it looked just like a four-leaf clover.

"Shhhh!" I told Ryan. "Don't tell anybody."

"You're pathetic, man," Ryan said.

"I found one!" I shouted. "I found a four-leaf clover!"

Everybody came running over and gathered around to see my four-leaf clover.

"Wow," said Mr. O'Loring. "Nice work, A.J.! That means you're going to have good luck for the rest of the day."

"Maybe I'll catch a leprechaun," I said, "and he'll give me his pot of gold at the end of a rainbow."

Ha! I should get the Nobel Prize for coming up with that idea.

That's a prize they give out to people who don't have bells. Ryan looked at me and shook his head.

Everybody else was excited about my four-leaf clover, and they all got back on their hands and knees so they could find one too. That's when the weirdest thing in the history of the world happened. While everybody was staring at the grass, I noticed somebody in the distance running near the back of the school.

I only saw him for a second. It looked like a little man. He was dressed in green, with a green hat.

"Hey, look!" I shouted.

"Where?" Neil asked.

"Over there!" I shouted, pointing at the door to the gym.

The little man pulled open the door and ran into the school.

"Who was that?" asked Alexia.

Michael said, "I think it was . . . a leprechaun!"

Larry the Leprechaun

WHAT?! A LEPRECHAUN? I thought leprechauns weren't real.

Everybody stopped looking for four-leaf clovers. We all started yelling and screaming and hooting and hollering and freaking out.

"Grab him!" Alexia shouted. "If we catch

him, he'll give us his pot of gold!"

We didn't bother lining up like Pringles. We just ran into the school.

"Which way did he go?" shouted Neil.

"This way!" Michael shouted. "Follow me!"

We ran down the hallway past the gym, the band room, and the all-porpoise room. I don't know why they call it the all-porpoise room. There are no dolphins in there. But there were no leprechauns in there either.

"He must be hiding *somewhere*!" shouted Emily.

We ran past the front office, the nurse's office, and the art room, looking up and down all the hallways. No leprechaun.

"He got away," said Alexia.

"Maybe he's hiding in the teachers' lounge!" shouted Ryan.

"Good thinking!" I shouted. "We're not allowed in there!"

We ran down the hall to the teachers' lounge. It's a magical wonderland where the teachers get back rubs, lie around in hot tubs, and have servants feed them grapes all day.*

I opened the door. Mr. O'Cooper was

---

*Or so they say.

sitting there at a table by himself. It looked like he was grading papers. I didn't see any hot tub or massage table.

"Students aren't allowed in the teachers' lounge," Mr. O'Cooper told us. "You kids know that."

"Did a leprechaun run in here?" I shouted.

"No, why?" asked Mr. O'Cooper.

"We were out in the playground," said Michael, "and we saw a leprechaun run in through the back door. Now we can't find him."

"A leprechaun in the school?!" shouted Mr. O'Cooper. "He may be in our classroom!"

He jumped up from his chair and ran out of the teachers' lounge. We all followed him. By the time we got to our classroom, I was panting. That means I was wearing pants.

Mr. O'Cooper yanked open the door. And you'll never believe in a million hundred years what we found in there.

A mess!

All our desks and chairs were upside down. Books and papers and colored pencils were scattered around. Our backpacks had been taken out of our cubbies and thrown on the floor.

"What happened?" asked Emily. "Was there a robbery?"

"No, this is what leprechauns do," said Mr. O'Cooper. "They play tricks on you."

"Man, leprechauns are slobs," I said.

Mr. O'Cooper looked angry. He likes a really neat classroom.

I noticed something on the floor near the door. It was a tiny envelope.

"Look!" I said as I ran over to pick it up. "It's a note!"

I gave the envelope to Mr. O'Cooper, and he tore it open. We all crowded around him as he read it. This is what it said . . .

Eeh eeh eeh
!em hctac t'nac uoY
nuahcerpeL eht yrraL—

"What does *that* mean?" asked Emily.

"Leprechauns are tricky," said Mr. O'Cooper. "He wrote it in code."

"Maybe he reversed the letters!" shouted Neil.

We read the note backward. This is what it said . . .

Hee hee hee
You can't catch me!
—Larry the Leprechaun

Larry the Leprechaun! At least now we had his name. But we didn't know where he was hiding.

"What are we gonna do?" asked Ryan.

"There's only one thing we *can* do," replied Mr. O'Cooper. "We need to make a leprechaun trap."

Green Food Is Gross

Yes! A leprechaun trap! If we could trap Larry the Leprechaun, we would get his pot of gold.

"But first we have to clean up this mess," said Mr. O'Cooper.

Bummer in the summer! Making a mess is fun, but cleaning up a mess is no fun at all. We spent a million hundred minutes picking up all the stuff off the floor and turning our desks and chairs right side up again. By the time we were finished getting the classroom in order, it was time for lunch. We would have to wait to make our leprechaun trap.

We pringled up and walked a million hundred miles to the vomitorium. It used to be called the "cafetorium," until some first grader threw up in there last year. Ever since then everybody calls it the vomitorium. Mrs. Patty was greeting kids at the door.

"Do you want to touch Jake the Snake?" she was asking everybody.

"We already touched him," Emily reminded her.

Sheesh, Mrs. Patty sure is obsessed with that snake.

"I'm so hungry," I said as we got in line. "I could eat a hundred slices of pizza."

"I could eat a *million* slices of pizza," said Ryan.

"I could eat a *trillion* slices of pizza," said Michael.

But there were no slices of pizza to eat. When we got to the front of the line, we saw our lunch lady, Ms. Hall. I mean, Ms. O'Hall.

"What would you like for lunch?" she asked cheerfully. "I've got green beans, green bread, green eggs, green muffins, green milk, green cupcakes, green dough- nuts, green pancakes with green syrup . . . and corned beef and cabbage."

I thought I was gonna throw up.

"Is the corned beef and cabbage green?" I asked.

"Ugh, no!" said Ms. O'Hall. "That would be gross!"

If you ask me, *any* food that's green is gross. I couldn't make up my mind what to eat.

"Why don't you start with some potatoes, A.J.?" Ms. O'Hall suggested.

"In honor of Saint Patrick's Day, I made baked potatoes, mashed potatoes, sweet potatoes, hash brown potatoes . . ."

I wanted to go to Antarctica and live with the penguins. Penguins don't have to eat green food and potatoes.

". . . garlic roasted potatoes, French fried potatoes, grilled potatoes, potato skins, potato soup, potato pancakes, potato salad . . ."*

---

*In case you were wondering, they eat a lot of potatoes in Ireland.

"Do you have anything that doesn't have potato in it?" I asked Ms. O'Hall.

"Well, the potato soup doesn't have *much* potato in it," she replied.

I took some corned beef and cabbage and sat down at a long table with everybody else. They were arguing about whether or not leprechauns were real.

"Larry the Leprechaun is probably just one of the teachers in disguise," said Neil. "I bet he's Mrs. O'Roopy. She's always dressing up like other people."

"I say leprechauns are real," said Ryan. "They wouldn't put them on cereal boxes if they weren't real."

"Don't leprechauns make shoes or

something?" asked Neil.

"I thought they made cookies," said Alexia.

"No, elves make cookies," said Michael. "Leprechauns make shoes."

"How do you get a pot of gold by making shoes?" I asked. "I don't think shoemakers make a lot of money."

"Yeah," added Emily, "and if leprechauns make shoes, how come there are no leprechaun shoe stores?"

Good point.

"If I got a pot of gold," said Alexia, "I would use the money to take a trip around the world."

"I would buy a new video game system,"

said Michael.

"I would put it in the bank," said Emily, "and use it to pay for college."

"I would buy all the candy in the world," said Neil.

"I would buy another pot of gold," I said. "So then I'd have *two* pots of gold."

I should get another Nobel Prize for that idea.

"That makes no sense, A.J.," said Ryan. "If you used your pot of gold to buy a pot of gold, you wouldn't have the first pot of gold anymore."

"Yeah," agreed Neil. "You wouldn't have more gold. You'd just have a different pot."

"That's right," said Alexia. "That would be like using four quarters to buy a dollar bill."

They were right. It was a dumb idea.

It had started raining, so we had indoor recess. Boo! Indoor recess is no fun. We walked a million hundred miles back to our classroom. But when we got there, we saw the weirdest thing in the history of the world.

The door was blocked by green ribbons.

We ripped them off and opened the door. And do you know what we found in there?

Green handprints. They were all over the place—on the floor, on the windows, and even on the walls. On the whiteboard in the front of the room, there was a message . . .

Sorry for the tricks and trouble
I had to leave here on the double.
I'll see you all another day
With lots more tricks I need to play.

Larry the Leprechaun had struck *again*!

When Mr. O'Cooper walked into the room and saw the handprints all over the place, he looked really mad.

"This means war!" he said.

Building a Leprechaun Trap

The war would have to wait, because it was time for art class. We had to walk a million hundred miles to the art room. Our teacher is Ms. Hannah. I mean, Ms. O'Hannah.

"In honor of Saint Patrick's Day," she told us, "I thought it would be fun to cut shamrocks out of construction paper and decorate the walls of the school with them."

There were sheets of green paper and scissors out on the table.

"Ms. O'Hannah," I said, "can we make a leprechaun trap instead?"

"Yeah," said Alexia. "If we catch Larry the Leprechaun, we'll get his pot of gold."

"What a *wonderful* idea!" said Ms. O'Hannah.

She cleared the paper off the table and got a bunch of other stuff—Popsicle sticks, string, tape, stickers, green tissue paper, a glue stick, and a big cardboard box.

She helped us cut a hole in the top of the cardboard box. Then we covered the hole with the tissue paper and the rest of the box with green paper. We glued a long stick to the side of the box and attached a string to the end of it so a fake gold coin would dangle over the hole. That would be the bait.

Finally, we made a little ladder out of Popsicle sticks so the leprechaun could climb up on the box and fall into the hole when he tried to grab the coin.

When our leprechaun trap was done, we stepped back to admire our work.

"It's cool," said Ryan.

"It's awesome," said Michael.

"It's sure to catch Larry the Leprechaun," said Alexia.

Ms. O'Hannah said we could take the

leprechaun trap back to our classroom. We walked a million hundred miles back there and set it up on a desk in the front of the room. And you'll never believe who walked into the door at that moment.

Nobody! People don't walk into doors! You'd bump your head.*

But you'll never believe who walked into the door*way*. It was our school tech guy, Mr. Harrison. I mean, Mr. O'Harrison.

Mr. O'Harrison fixes the computers and copy machines when they break down. He can fix anything.

"What's that contraption?" asked Mr. O'Harrison.

---

*Don't you ever learn?

"It's a leprechaun trap," said Mr. O'Cooper. "The students just built it during art class."

Mr. O'Harrison walked around the trap, looking it over. Then he let out a snort.

"You call *that* a leprechaun trap?" he said. "That's not gonna catch any leprechauns."

"It won't?" we all said.

"Nah," said Mr. O'Harrison. "For one thing, it's too small."

He was probably right. The leprechaun I saw running into the school was way too big to fit inside our trap.

"I'll be back in a jiff," said Mr. O'Harrison as he ran out of the room.

I don't know what peanut butter had to do with anything. But a few minutes later Mr. O'Harrison came back. He was pushing a big cart full of wood, a hammer, nails, and lots of other stuff, including a big bell that looked like the Liberty Bell.

"Leprechauns are tricky and sneaky," Mr. O'Harrison told us. "If you want to catch 'em, you've got to be trickier and sneakier than they are."

He unrolled a big sheet of paper on

Mr. O'Cooper's desk. It had a drawing of a leprechaun trap on it. We all gathered around him as he explained how it worked.

"Look," Mr. O'Harrison said as he pointed to his drawing. "First, we lure the leprechaun over *here* with some cookies and gold coins. When he steps on *this* spot, he'll bump against this string. That will knock over this line of dominoes. The last domino will hit this little car. It will roll down this ramp and bump into the baseball at the end. The baseball will roll down this tube and push this box of rocks off the table. The box of rocks will land on this bicycle pedal and turn it, causing these nails to pop the water balloon. The

Leprechaun

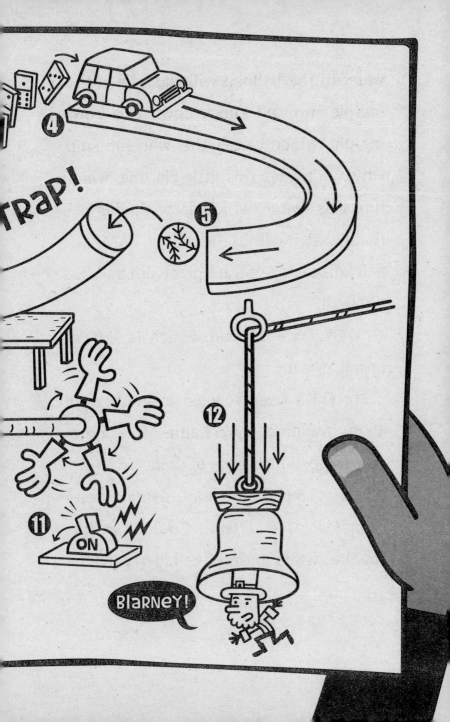

water in the balloon will slide down this marble run and knock down this bowling pin, which causes this wheel to spin, which activates this little zip line, which flips this switch, which drops the big bell that's hanging from the ceiling. BAM! The bell falls on top of the leprechaun and he's trapped!"

"WOW," we all said, which is "MOM" upside down.

Mr. O'Harrison seemed to know a lot about trapping leprechauns. He's probably trapped hundreds of them.

"That leprechaun trap seems pretty complicated," said Ryan. "Couldn't we just flip the switch to drop the Liberty Bell on the leprechaun?"

"No," said Mr. O'Harrison.

"Couldn't we just shoot the leprechaun with a tranquilizer dart?" asked Alexia. "Or throw a big net over him?"

"No!" said Mr. O'Harrison. "No self-respecting leprechaun is going to fall for that."

We started building Mr. O'Harrison's leprechaun trap. It was hard work, and it took a million hundred hours. Attaching the big Liberty Bell to the ceiling with a rope was the hardest part. That bell is really heavy. We all had to work together to pick it up.

"Where do you think Mr. O'Harrison

got this Liberty Bell?" Ryan asked me as we were hoisting it up to the ceiling.

"From Rent-a-Liberty-Bell," I replied. "You can rent anything."

When we were finished, we scattered some cookies and gold coins around the floor to lure Larry the Leprechaun into our trap. Alexia made a sign that said FREE GOLD and put it next to the coins. We stepped back to admire our work.

"There, it's done," said Mr. O'Harrison. "*This* is how you catch yourself a leprechaun!"

"It's cool," said Ryan.

"It's awesome," said Michael.

"It's sure to catch Larry the Leprechaun,"

said Alexia. "Do you think we should paint it green?"

"Nah!" said Mr. O'Harrison. "That's what leprechauns *expect*. You've got to fool them if you want to catch them."

Free gold

Proof

After Mr. O'Harrison left, it was time for us to go to science class. We walked a million hundred miles to the science lab. In the hallway, we saw Mrs. Patty with her snake basket again.

"Would you like to touch Jake the Snake?" she asked us.

"We already did that!" Ryan reminded her.

"He's my baby," said Mrs. Patty.

Sheesh! Mrs. Patty should give it a rest with that snake already.

Our science teacher is Mr. Docker. I mean, Mr. O'Docker. You'll never believe what weird thing he was doing when we walked into the science lab.

I'm not going to tell you.

Okay, okay, I'll tell you. He was peeling potatoes!

I *told* you it was weird. Mr. O'Docker is off his o'rocker! He was sitting there with two big buckets in front of him. One was filled with the potatoes he'd already peeled, and the other one had the potatoes he hadn't peeled yet.

"Mr. O'Docker," said Alexia. "Why are you peeling potatoes?"

"I need them for my car," he replied.

Oh, yeah. Mr. O'Docker has a car that doesn't use gas or electricity. It runs on potato power.* That's weird. After lunch, there must have been lots of extra potatoes in the vomitorium, so Mr. O'Docker was able to get some to use in his car.

"It's Saint Patrick's Day," he told us, "so let's talk about the science of the color green . . ."

---

*You can read all about it in *My Weird School #10: Mr. Docker Is Off His Rocker!*

Oh no. We had to learn more stuff.

"Green is a very interesting color," said Mr. O'Docker. "It's between blue and yellow on the visible spectrum and *blah blah blah blah* photosynthesis *blah blah blah blah* camouflage *blah blah blah blah* environment *blah blah blah blah . . .*"

He went on like that for a million hundred hours talking about the color green. What a snoozefest!

Mr. O'Docker knows a lot about science. I bet he could build an awesome leprechaun trap.

"Did you ever build a leprechaun trap, Mr. O'Docker?" I asked.

He shook his head and made a little frown.

"I hate to be the one to tell you kids this," he replied, "but leprechauns don't exist in the real world. They're just imaginary creatures, like fairies and elves."

Wait. Fairies and elves aren't real? Who knew?

Mr. O'Docker explained that scientists don't believe in things unless they have proof. He told us about something called the scientific method, which is how scientists prove what's true and what isn't. He went on for a million hundred hours explaining the scientific method.

"Blah blah blah blah . . ."

I had no idea what he was talking about. Finally, Mr. O'Docker stopped talking.

"Any questions?" he asked.

"Yes," I said, raising my hand. "Can I go to the bathroom?"

"I don't know, A.J.," said Mr. O'Docker. "*Can* you go to the bathroom?"

Oh, I keep forgetting. We're not supposed to say, "Can I go to the bathroom?" We're supposed to say, "*May* I go to the bathroom?" Nobody knows why.

"*May* I go to the bathroom?" I asked.

"Certainly, A.J."

Mr. O'Docker said we could take a

bathroom break before going back to class. Ryan and I went to the boys' bathroom, which is right across the hall from the science room. I went into one of the stalls. And you'll never believe what I found in there.

If you guessed "a toilet," you're right! Of *course* there was a toilet in the stall. What else would you find in a bathroom stall?

But it just so happens that there *was* something else in the stall. On the wall above the toilet, somebody had written words in green glitter . . .

Tricky, tricky, you tried to be.
Try again, you won't catch me!

I looked down. On the toilet seat, there were two small green footprints.

Then I looked in the toilet. The water... was *green*!

WHAT?! Larry the Leprechaun must have peed in our toilet!

"AHHHHHHH!" I screamed.

Ryan was washing his hands at the sink. He came running over.

"What's the matter?" he asked. "Did you fall into the toilet bowl?"

"No!" I shouted. "Larry the Leprechaun peed in it!"

"That's proof that leprechauns exist!" said Ryan. "Their pee must be green!"

"Larry the Leprechaun should remember to flush," I said.

We checked the other stalls. None of them had green pee in them, but one had a bunch of jelly beans on the floor.

"Why would a leprechaun scatter jelly beans on the floor?" Ryan asked.

"Those aren't jelly beans!" I shouted.

"They're leprechaun poops!"

"AHHHHHHH!" we both screamed.

We ran out of the boys' bathroom in a panic. Alexia and Emily were in the hallway ahead of us.

"A leprechaun peed in the girls' bathroom!" Alexia shouted.

"AHHHHHHH!"

"That means there's more than one leprechaun!" yelled Ryan.

"Maybe they're a husband-and-wife leprechaun team!" hollered Emily.

We ran into the science room to tell Mr. O'Docker the big news.

"Leprechauns are peeing and pooping in the bathrooms!" I shouted.

"This proves that leprechauns are real!" said Alexia.

"Yeah," said Emily. "We used the scientific method."

Mr. O'Docker wasn't convinced.

"Did any of you actually *see* a leprechaun in the bathroom?" asked Mr. O'Docker.

"No," we admitted.

"Did you *hear* a leprechaun in the bathroom?"

"No."

"Then you don't have proof," said Mr. O'Docker. "A scientist will do careful experiments before coming to a conclusion. Let me know when you find some *real* proof."

We walked a million hundred miles back to class.

"I don't care what Mr. O'Docker says," Alexia whispered. "I think leprechauns are real."

"Yeah," I agreed. "Science teachers don't know everything."

We were just about to enter our classroom when the weirdest thing in the history of the world happened. Mrs. Patty was outside our door. She looked upset.

"Jake the Snake . . ." she began.

"We told you a million hundred times," I said. "We already touched your snake. We don't want to touch him again."

Mrs. Patty started crying. That was weird.

"You *can't* touch him!" she sobbed. "Jake the Snake is *missing*!"

The Big
Surprise Ending

Mrs. Patty looked really upset. Tears were running down her face. She managed to tell us that Jake the Snake had somehow slithered out of his basket and was gone.

"Where could he be?" asked Emily.

"If I knew that, he wouldn't be missing!" said Mrs. Patty, sobbing.

All of us looked at the floor at the same time. If Jake the Snake was missing, that meant he could be *anywhere*. He could be right next to our feet. He could be about to bite our toes off! He could be . . .

"AHHHHHHHHHH!"

Suddenly, everybody was yelling and screaming and hooting and hollering and freaking out.

"There's nothing to be afraid of!" Mrs. Patty shouted. "Jake the Snake is harmless! He's an eastern hognose."

I didn't care what kind of a hognose he was. I didn't want a snake biting my toes off. We ran inside our classroom and climbed up on our desks so Jake the Snake wouldn't be able to get at us.

Once we were up on our desks, I noticed something weird. The Liberty Bell wasn't hanging from the ceiling anymore. It was on the floor. And there was a muffled noise coming out of it.

"Look!" I shouted, as I pointed at the Liberty Bell. "Jake the Snake must have set off our trap! He's inside the bell!"

Everybody looked at the Liberty Bell.

"Jake!" shouted Mrs. Patty. "My baby!"

That's when the weirdest thing in the history of the world happened. I heard *another* noise coming from inside the Liberty Bell. And I'm pretty sure it wasn't Jake the Snake.

"Help! Help!" cried a muffled voice. "Let me out of here!"

"It's not Jake the Snake!" I shouted. "It's Larry the Leprechaun!"

"WE CAUGHT HIM!" everyone shouted at once.

We all jumped down from our desks and ran over to the Liberty Bell.

"Okay," said Alexia. "Let's pick it up."

"Get ready to grab him as soon as the bell is off the floor," said Ryan. "Remember, he's fast, and he's tricky."

All of us gathered around the Liberty Bell. It was really heavy.

We groaned and moaned trying to pick it up. We couldn't wait to see what Larry the Leprechaun looked like. Everybody was on pins and needles.

Well, not really. It would hurt to be on pins and needles.

But there was electricity in the air.

Well, not exactly. If there was electricity

in the air, we would have been electro-cuted. But we were all glued to our seats.

Well, no. That would be weird. Why would I glue myself to a seat? How would I get the glue off my pants?

But it was intense.*

Slowly, the Liberty Bell started to rise.

Isn't this exciting?

And you'll never believe in a million hundred years what was under the Liberty Bell.

I'm not going to tell you.

Okay, okay, I'll tell you.

IT WAS ANDREA YOUNG!

---

*We weren't in tents! What did tents have to do with anything? We weren't camping.

Betcha didn't see *that* coming! Andrea was dressed up like a leprechaun! She even had a beard.

"EEEEEK!" Andrea screamed, running out from under the Liberty Bell.

"EEEEEK!" we all screamed as we put it down.

"Andrea!" shouted Emily as the two girls hugged. "I thought you didn't like Saint Patrick's Day."

"Yeah," I said. "What are *you* doing here? We thought you were girlcotting Saint Patrick's Day."

"I couldn't stay home!" Andrea told us. "I didn't want to miss all the fun you guys were having without me. Mr. O'Klutz said

I could come to school dressed up like a leprechaun."

"Nice beard," Michael said as Andrea pulled off her beard.

"So *you* were the one who turned our desks upside down and messed up the classroom?" asked Ryan.

"Yes," Andrea admitted.

"And *you* were the one who wrote those messages?" asked Alexia.

"Guilty as charged," Andrea replied.

"And *you* were the one who peed and pooped in the toilets?" I asked.

"It was just food coloring and jelly beans, Arlo," she said. "I *told* you leprechauns aren't real."

"The leprechaun is finally gone!" said Emily.

All my life, I've been waiting for something to fall on Andrea's head. Finally, something did!

I was going to say something mean to her, but I didn't get the chance. Some kids were shouting in the hallway. We all ran out to see what was going on.

"EEEEEEEK!" somebody screamed. "It's a snake!"

It was true. Jake the Snake was slithering around the hallway outside our room. Lots of kids were yelling and screaming and hooting and hollering and freaking out. We saw it live and in person.

"Run for your lives!" shouted Neil.

You should have *been* there! Kids were diving out of the way and crashing into each other. Jake the Snake was slithering back and forth really fast. I think he was just as scared as we were.

That's when Mr. O'Klutz came running over. He was carrying a broom and wearing hip waders, those weird rubber pants that fishermen wear so they don't get wet.

"Everyone remain calm!" he shouted. "Let me handle this!"

Mr. O'Klutz started chasing Jake the Snake with the broom.

"Don't hurt him!" shouted Mrs. Patty. "He's my baby! Be careful!"

"I'll catch him!" Mr. O'Klutz shouted. "Don't worry!"

But Mr. O'Klutz didn't catch him. Jake the Snake slithered down the hallway. Mr. O'Klutz was right behind, chasing him.

"Jake!" shouted Mrs. Patty. "Come back, sweetheart!"

They couldn't catch him. Jake slithered right out the door, into the playground, and out to the woods behind the school. We never saw him again.

Well, that's pretty much what happened on Saint Patrick's Day. Maybe you get *bad* luck when you take a three-leaf clover and pretend it's a four-leaf clover. I didn't see any rainbow and I didn't get any pot of gold. Everybody was upset that Larry the

Leprechaun was just Andrea in disguise.

We never did get around to researching whether or not Saint Patrick drove the snakes out of Ireland. But we *do* know that Mr. O'Klutz drove a snake out of Ella Mentry School. And that's pretty impressive, if you ask me. Maybe from now on we'll call Saint Patrick's Day "Mr. Klutz Day."

Maybe Mrs. Patty will be able to capture Jake the Snake. Maybe he will eat a first grader for lunch. Maybe Larry the Leprechaun will remember to flush the toilet. Maybe girlcott will become a word. Maybe we'll find out what Pickle-Palooza is. Maybe Andrea will get a sense of humor transplant. Maybe leprechauns will open shoe stores. Maybe now that you've finished this book, you'll read a magic chicken.

But it won't be easy!

The Leprechaun Is Finally Gone!

MY WeiRd School Special

WEIRD EXTRAS!

- Weird Stuff You Probably Don't Know about Ireland

- My Weird School from A to Z

- Fun Games and Weird Word Puzzles

- The World of Dan Gutman Checklist

WEIRD STUFF YOU PROBABLY DON'T KNOW ABOUT IRELAND

 Professor A.J. here. I know everything about Saint Patrick's Day and Ireland. That's why they call me "professor."

Nobody calls you that, dumbhead! I'll bet you didn't even know that Saint Patrick wasn't born in Ireland. He was born in Wales.

 He was born in a whale? That's weird. How did he get out?

Very funny, Arlo. In fact, Saint Patrick's

name wasn't even Patrick. It was Maewyn Succat.

What?! If my name was Maewyn Succat, I'd change it to Patrick too.

Arlo, you don't know *anything* about Ireland, do you?

Sure, I do. I know plenty of stuff. Like, if somebody in Ireland asks where the "jacks" is, that means they want to know where the toilet is.

That's inappropriate for children, Arlo.

Toilets are inappropriate for children? Then where do they go to the bathroom?

 Ugh, you're impossible. Look, why don't you go play video games or something while I tell the readers about Ireland?

 Sounds good to me. I'm sure it will be a snoozefest.

I did some research . . .

Ugh, research.

. . . and I discovered some really interesting facts about Ireland. This is what I found.

- The longest place name in Ireland is the town of Muckanaghederdauhaulia. It means "a ridge, shaped like a pig's back, between two expanses of briny water."

- Ireland is the only country that has a musical instrument—the harp—as its national symbol.

- Halloween began in Ireland. It marked the end of the harvest season and the beginning of winter.

- Here are some famous people from Ireland you've probably never heard of: The submarine was invented by John Philip Holland. The first immigrant to enter the United States through Ellis Island on January 1, 1892 was Annie Moore from Cork, Ireland. James Hoban designed the White House in Washington, DC. And a scientist named John Tyndall is credited with explaining why the sky is blue.
- The one of the oldest working lighthouses in the world is Hook Lighthouse in Ireland. It was built around 1200 CE.
- Sir Walter Raleigh was a British explorer who is said to have planted the first

potato in Ireland around 1589. He brought the potato crop from the Americas.

- Before it sank, the *Titanic* sailed from Ireland.
- The game of hurling, which is said to be the world's fastest game played on grass, was invented in Ireland more than 3,000 years ago. It's sort of a combination of soccer, lacrosse, and baseball.
- Every year in Chicago on Saint Patrick's

Day, forty pounds of dye is dumped into the Chicago River to turn it green.

- The song "When Irish Eyes Are Smiling" was written by two Americans, George Graff Jr. and Chauncey Olcott. They'd never even visited Ireland!

- In celebration of Saint Patrick's Day in 2013, astronaut Chris Hadfield took photos of Ireland and photos of himself wearing green in the International Space Station. He also posted recordings of himself singing the song "Danny Boy" in space.

- You may not want to go to Ireland on your birthday. It's a tradition there to pick kids up, turn them upside down,

and tap their head on the floor the number of their age plus one.

- Every August in Killorglin, Ireland, they have a festival in which a wild goat is caught, put in a cage, and crowned king for three days. After the festival is over, the goat is set free.

 That's weird. Are you finished?

Yes!

MY WEIRD SCHOOL
FROM A TO Z

A.J. and Andrea: Two main characters. They hate each other and are secretly in love, love, *love*!

All-Porpoise Room: Room at school where dolphins are kept.

Bathroom: To make your friends laugh, stick your face in their face and say this word. *See also* **Underwear**.

Boring: What just about everything is, except for skateboarding, peewee football, trick biking, video games, and cool stuff like that.

But it won't be easy: The final sentence of every My Weird School book.

Candy: The greatest thing in the history of the world.

Clog dancing: A dance that plumbers do.

Dictionary: A big fat book with a lot of words in it, and it's in alphabetical order. Andrea keeps one on her desk at all times so she can look up words and make sure she's smarter than everybody else.

Door holder: Somebody whose job it is to hold the door open. So it has the perfect name.

Dumbhead: The worst curse word in the world.

Ella Mentry: The old lady who lives nearby and taught at the school for many years. After she retired, the school was named "Ella Mentry School."

Fiction: What you get when you rub two things together. Oh, wait a minute. That's friction. Never mind.

Finger painting: When you paint your fingers. What a dumb thing to do.

Fizz Ed: The only good thing about school, because it's what you would be doing if you didn't have to go there in the first place.

Forehead: Grown-ups rub theirs when they're thinking. When you get old, your brain doesn't work as well anymore so you have to rub your forehead to get it going again.

Grown-ups: Old people. They invented school as a way to avoid paying for babysitters.

Hips: Where grown-ups put their hands when they're mad. Nobody knows why.

Hmmm: What grown-ups say instead of "er" or "um" or "uh" when they don't know what to say.

Hold your tongue: Something grown-ups are always telling you to do. But it's slimy and gross.

I'll be your best friend: All-purpose promise used to get anything from anyone.

Jack: The first extreme athlete. He was some guy who would jump over a candlestick for no reason.

Jill: Friend of Jack.

Kinetic sculpture: Sculpture that comes from Connecticut.

Last straw, the: Something grown-ups always say to A.J., even though he didn't take any straws and there are plenty of straws left.

Line leader: Kid who gets the honor of walking at the head of the class when it moves from room to room.

Lumpy: Humpty Dumpty's actual first name.

Math: Stuff kids have to learn even though there are calculators that can do it for you.

Mature: A fancy way to say boring.

Million hundred: A.J.'s way of saying any large number.

Motto: What's a motto? I don't know. What's a motto with you?

Nah-nah-nah boo-boo: What you say after you won and somebody else lost.

Nonfiction: Books that don't have any fiction in them, just like nonfat milk doesn't have fat in it and nonsense doesn't have sense in it.

O: Letter you put in front of your name on Saint Patrick's Day so you sound Irish.

Paper: Stuff that all My Weird School books are printed on. Except the ebook and audio versions.

Paillot, Jim: Some guy who draws pictures.

Pudding: What the proof is in.

Reading and writing: Boring stuff that has no place in schools.

Recess: The best time of the day.

Skateboarding: One of A.J.'s favorite sports. The first picture in the first My Weird School book shows A.J. skateboarding.

Teachers' lounge: A secret place where teachers have parties all day long. They dance around, eat cake, get massages, and think up new ways to punish kids. Oh, and they have a hot tub in there.

The: A word found on just about every page of every book in the history of the world. Nobody knows why.

TV: Valuable educational tool that gives us kids important information, like which breakfast cereal tastes best and which shampoo leaves your hair the shiniest.

Underwear: To make your friends laugh, stick your face in their face and say this word. *See also* **Bathroom**.

Veterinarian: What Andrea wants to be when she grows up, even though animals can't be doctors.

Vomitorium: The lunchroom. It used to be called the "cafetorium" until some first grader threw up in there.

Weather: What grown-ups talk about all the time, usually while drinking coffee. Nobody knows why.

Whistling: What you do when you want to pretend you didn't do anything wrong, even though everybody knows you did that thing.

X-rays: Miss Small got these after she fell out of a tree and broke her leg.

You can't come to my birthday party: Just about the meanest thing you can say to somebody.

Zamboni: Used at hockey games. It has nothing to do with My Weird School, but it's a funny word that starts with a Z.

FUN GAMES AND WEIRD WORD PUZZLES

LUCK OF THE IRISH

Directions: Help Andrea navigate this maze to reach the pot of gold at the end of the rainbow!

SPOT THE DIFFERENCES

Directions: These two covers are identical. Well, *almost*. There are ten differences. Can you spot them all?

New York Times Bestselling Author

Dan Gutman

My WeiRd School SpeciaL!

The Leprechaun Is Finally Gone!

EXTRAS
GaMeS! PuzzLeS!
aND MoRe!

Pictures by
Jim Paillot

SAINT PATTY'S CROSSWORD

Directions: Use the clues below to fill in this crossword puzzle. (Hint: All of the answers are mentioned in this book!)

Across:

5. _____ are known for wearing green and playing pranks on people.

6. A type of Irish dancing performed on Saint Patrick's Day.

7. The number of leaves a lucky clover has.

9. The country where Saint Patrick was born.

10. This is traditionally worn by the Scottish and often mistaken for a skirt.

Down:

1. What people think the Irish eat a lot of on Saint Patrick's Day.

2. A pot of this can be found at the end of a rainbow.

3. A three-leaf clover is also known as this.

4. Saint Patrick's Day is always on March ___.

8. Ireland's national symbol is this musical instrument.

HIDDEN WORD HUNT

Directions: Can you find all ten Saint Patrick's Day words hidden in this messy jumble of letters?

```
C X O D K P A Z P I V V F H P
E R A I N B O W H W O L F S H
E F W A L O Q S Y D J W N H J
D B U X O E F Z G R E E N A A
K S R K J X P Q M A R C H M S
K M D D J O A R M E B S T R V
V H X J M X M S E O M B I O E
D Y A C Y Z K A W C K V Z C U
L N T Y L O W I Q F H F K K M
U W G D Z O L N I N B A D N T
C K P K L L V T J I S L U E A
K W T G N N K E V E Q G G N I
I H M U E D Y S R I R I S H X
K A D U R K W R G S H I X T V
Y T Q G O L D G F C L A T B D
```

LEPRECHAUN SHAMROCK
RAINBOW GREEN CLOVER
SAINT MARCH GOLD IRISH LUCK

ANSWER KEY

LUCK OF THE IRISH

SPOT THE DIFFERENCES

SAINT PATTY'S CROSSWORD

HIDDEN WORD HUNT

C X O D K P A Z P I V V F H P
E R A I N B O W H W O L F S H
E F W A L O Q S Y D J W N H J
D B U X O E F Z G R E E N A A
K S R K J X P Q M A R C H M S
K M D D J O A R M E B S T R V
V H X J M X M S E O M B I O E
D Y A C Y Z K A W C K V Z C U
L N T Y L Q W I Q F H F K K M
U W G D Z O L N I N B A D N T
C K P K L L V T J I S L U E A
K W T G N N K E V E Q G G N I
I H M U E D Y S R I R I S H X
K A D U R K W R G S H I X T V
Y T Q G O L D G F C L A T B D

THE WORLD OF DAN GUTMAN CHECKLIST

MY WEIRD SCHOOL

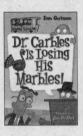

MY WEIRD SCHOOL DAZE

MY WEIRDER SCHOOL

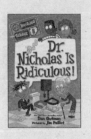

MY WEIRD SCHOOL SPECIAL

MY WEIRDEST SCHOOL

MY WEIRDER-EST SCHOOL

MY WEIRD SCHOOL FAST FACTS

   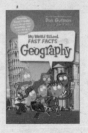

MY WEIRD SCHOOL GRAPHIC NOVELS

MY WEIRD TIPS

MY WEIRD SCHOOL
JOKES, GAMES, AND PUZZLES

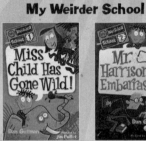